This book belongs to

....

For Mr Roger Bear,
much love – J.N.

EGMONT
We bring stories to life

First published in Great Britain 2011 by Egmont UK Limited
This edition published 2018 by Dean,
an imprint of Egmont UK Limited,
The Yellow Building, 1 Nicholas Road, London, W11 4AN
www.egmont.co.uk

Text and illustration copyright © Jill Newton 2011
The moral rights of the author/illustrator have been asserted

ISBN 978 0 6035 7573 0

70173/001

Printed in Malaysia

A CIP catalogue record for this title is available from the
British Library.

Stay safe online. Egmont is not responsible for content hosted
by third parties.

Egmont takes its responsibility to the planet and its inhabitants
very seriously. All the papers we use are from well-managed
forests run by responsible suppliers.

DON'T WAKE MR BEAR!

Jill Newton

EGMONT

Down in the wood,
between two oak trees,
a golden leaf

floated

to the

ground.

Ting!

Dormouse struck his triangle.
He was the leader of the Woodland Orchestra
and it was time for the lullaby of the forest to begin.

Dormouse gathered the orchestra together.
"Places, please," he said.

The squirrels sat in their trees
and blew the sound of the breeze.

Plink plonk plink!

The wood pigs tapped their xylophones
and the acorns dropped
from the trees.

Thrrrrrrrrrrrum!

The rabbits strummed
their harps as the leaves
fluttered down
around them.

And, remember, WHATEVER you do, don't wake Mr Bear!"

With that he went off to bed.

The gentle music was making
everyone, and everything,
feel very sleepy.

Until ...

Suddenly . . .

BANG!!

A carload of **wolves** crashed into a tree.
"HOWDY!" called one wolf,
tooting his horn.

"DO YOU WANT A PARTY?"
yelled another.

"Shhhh!" whispered
the squirrels.
"Be quiet! You'll wake
Mr Bear!"

But the wolves weren't listening.

Out of the car came
the wolves' **drums**,
and their **lights**,
and their **speakers**.

"Go away!" begged the rabbits.
"You'll wake Mr Bear!"

"We don't care
about a silly
old bear!"
sang the wolves.

Before long,
the **squirrels** and the **rabbits**
and the **wood pigs** didn't care
about Mr Bear either.

They were having
MUCH too
much fun!

Until . . .

"Uh-oh," said the squirrels.
"It's time for you to go!"

"You've woken
Mr Bear!"
said the rabbits.

"But we're
on holiday!"
protested
the wolves.

Mr Bear turned
towards the animals ...

"Don't be ridiculous!"
he said to them.
"If these chaps are on holiday,
we must show them a good time!"

Mr Bear grabbed a snazzy-looking shirt
and led the party,
dancing and stomping through
the forest all night,
creating the loudest
rumpus of all.

The sun had just started to rise when . . .

...there was a sudden

CRASH!

The party animals stopped
in their tracks.

There stood a very **tired**

and very **angry** . . .

"You told us not to
wake Mr Bear,"
they replied.

**"AND WHAT HAVE
YOU DONE?"**
he yelled at the squirrels.

"Woken Mr Bear," they said meekly.

**"AND WHAT
MADE YOU
WAKE MR BEAR?"**

The squirrels and rabbits
waited for the wolves to explain –
but the wolves were
nowhere to be seen.

Mr Bear bumbled over.
"Great timing little fellow.
Where's the food?
I'm feeling peckish."

"**FOOD!**
There **IS** no food,
you silly bear!
The forest is going to sleep,
just like you should be.
Without rest, the trees won'
grow any berries or nuts.
There'll be **NO** juicy bugs
to pick on. And how would
you feel then?" Dormouse shouted.

"Not very happy,"
mumbled Mr Bear.

"SO BE QUIET THEN
AND GO TO BED!"
shouted Dormouse.

Ting!

Dormouse struck his triangle.
The squirrels climbed up into their trees,
    the wood pigs tapped their xylophones
        and the rabbits picked up their harps.

The Woodland Orchestra played
the lullaby of the forest once more,
as Mr Bear yawned
and shuffled back off to his cave.

"**Perfect,**" yawned Dormouse. "**Perfect music for the long winter sleep. Just one more thing . . .**"

He turned to the wolves, hiding up in the trees. "**I'd like you lot to keep time, but quietly!**

After all, YOU **DON'T WANT TO WAKE** **MR DORMOUSE,** do you?"